# THE THISTLE PRIN

In this book you will find three original fairy stories. Each is full of memorable characters and magical events and is ideal for reading aloud.

Vivian French became a broadcast poet on *Children's Hour* at the tender age of six. Some years later, she worked in children's theatre, both as an actor and writer, and is now an author and storyteller. She has written many children's books, including *Zenobia and Mouse, Mary Poggs and the Sunshine* and another collection of original fairytales, *Under the Moon* (also illustrated by Chris Fisher). She is also the author of *A Song for Little Toad* (shortlisted for the 1995 Smarties Book Prize), *Lazy Jack, Princess Primrose* and several other picture books, as well as the Read and Wonder non-fiction titles *Caterpillar Caterpillar* (shortlisted for the 1993 Kurt Maschler Award), *The Apple Trees* and *Spider Watching*. She has four daughters, two cats and a guinea-pig and lives in Bristol.

Chris Fisher is the illustrator of the picture book *Princess Primrose*, the young fiction title *Pappy Mashy* (by Kathy Henderson) and a number of other children's stories.

*A small thistle was ... hidden among the willow's
arching roots. She shook her purple head and sniffed.*

# THE THISTLE PRINCESS

## and other stories

*Written by*
VIVIAN FRENCH

*Illustrated by*
CHRIS FISHER

WALKER BOOKS
AND SUBSIDIARIES
LONDON • BOSTON • SYDNEY

*For the children of*
*Oklahoma*

First published 1995 by Walker Books Ltd
87 Vauxhall Walk, London SE11 5HJ

This edition published 1996

2 4 6 8 10 9 7 5 3 1

Text © 1995 Vivian French
Illustrations © 1995 Chris Fisher

This book has been typeset in Plantin Light.

Printed in England

British Library Cataloguing in Publication Data
A catalogue record for this book
is available from the British Library.

ISBN 0-7445-4747-4

# CONTENTS

*Sometimes the queen would sit under the willow tree
... and cry.*

# THE THISTLE PRINCESS

Long, long ago, before time was caught and kept in clocks, there lived a king and a queen. They ruled their kingdom wisely and well, but they did not often smile. Sometimes the king would lean by the window and sigh, and sometimes the queen would sit under the willow tree in the royal garden and cry until the grass around her was wet with her tears.

"Why is she crying?" whispered the roses. "Why is she so sad?"

"We don't know," murmured the lilies and poppies and daisies. "We don't know."

The willow shook his great leafy head.

"Why does the king sit and sigh?" he asked. "Who knows? Not I."

A small thistle was growing close by, hidden among the willow's arching roots. She shook her purple head and sniffed.

"How silly they are," she said to herself. "It all comes of being so beautiful. They've got no sense, no sense at all. Anyone sensible could see that the king and the queen want a baby, a child, a little boy or girl to run about and laugh and keep them company from daybreak to sunset. Poof!" And she sniffed again.

If the willow heard her he took no notice. He was not in the habit of talking to thistles.

One day the gardener brought his youngest son to play in the garden.

"Excuse me for bringing him, Your Majesty," the gardener said, "but I thought as he'd like to see the flowers. He'll be no trouble."

The queen looked at the gardener's son and smiled. "He is most welcome," she said. "Let him play wherever he wishes." And all day she watched the little boy as he toddled this way and that, up and down the paths and in and out of the roses and poppies and lilies and daisies. The king, sitting at his window, watched as well … and he never sighed, not once.

"There!" said the little thistle, and she nodded to herself. "What have I been saying all along? What they need is a child of their own!"

That evening, as the stars were creeping up the purple sky, the willow rustled his leaves.

"Ahem," he said, and the roses opened their sleepy eyes. The poppies lifted their heavy heads, and the lilies whispered, "Wake up! Wake up!" to the daisies.

"Ahem," said the willow. "I know now why the king and the queen are so sad."

The flowers murmured and swayed to and fro.

"They are sad," the willow said, "because they have no children. While the gardener's child was here the queen was happy all day, and the king waved and smiled from his window."

The roses nodded. "We saw," they said, "we saw. But what can we do?"

The willow wept a tear or two and swept his long green fingers across the ground. "You have the softness of a baby's cheek," he said to the roses, "and the lilies have the sweetness of a baby's breath. The daisies are bright and the poppies are silken with deep dark eyes, and I myself can catch the singing of the birds... But what to do? What to do? What to do?" And he swayed and sighed, and the roses and the poppies and the lilies and the daisies swayed and sighed with him.

The little thistle could bear it no longer. She stood up straight.

"Never mind about the singing of the birds," she said. "What a willow is good for is baskets. Forget about the fancy words, old man willow – weave a fine cradle for the king and the queen, and then we'll see what's to do!"

There was instantly a rustling and fluttering of leaves and twigs and branches.

"A *weed*!" trembled the lilies. "A *weed* telling *us* what we should do!"

The poppies drew back in alarm, and the roses closed their petals up tightly. The willow quivered with indignation. Only the daisies looked at the thistle with their bright eyes and nodded to her.

"A baby?" they asked. "A baby? Can it be done?"

"It can!" said the thistle sternly. "Now, old man willow, are you all puff and pother and long words, or are you willing to help that poor lonely king and queen?"

The willow took a moment or two to decide. To be ordered about by a common thistle was a dreadful thing, but not to help the king and queen of all the kingdom was surely worse… The willow bowed his great green head, and the longest and most beautiful of his slender branches began to twist and weave in and out and out and in.

"That's better," said the thistle, and she turned to the beds of flowers. "Now, come along! We'll need some help from all of you as well!"

As the willow laid the green leafy cradle

gently on the grass, the roses leant tenderly over it and dropped pink and white and deep crimson petals inside. The lilies offered their golden fragrance, and the poppies their crumpled scarlet silk. The daisies shook in a scatter of bright whiteness, and the willow twitched his leaves to one side so that the falling cascade of song from an evening thrush slid in among the softness and sweetness.

"And what have *you* to offer?" the willow demanded of the thistle. "I hope you have no intention of adding your sharp needles and pins!"

The thistle sighed a little. "There has to be more than pretty leaves and petals," she said.

"H'mph!" said the willow. "We shall see what we shall see in the morning!" And he bowed to the admiring roses and lilies and poppies and daisies before he gathered his branches around him and slept.

The little thistle waited until all the flowers had closed their petals and the night was still. Then, slowly and painfully, she pulled herself up from the warm earth and laid herself down in the willow cradle. She could feel herself wilting and shrivelling as she sank into the scented petals. Her strong grey-green leaves withered and grew brittle, and her fine purple head turned to silver white.

"What needs doing must be done," she said, and never spoke again.

The willow was woken in the morning by a strange sound. It was coming from the cradle, and he peered through his long green fingers in amazement. There, lying in the basket of his own making, was a baby – a baby with the skin of rose petals and the sweetness of lilies, and bright eyes that shone as she gazed up into the leafy heaven above. She was wrapped in scarlet silk, and she kicked her little fat legs and crowed and laughed.

The queen was the next to hear the baby. She came running down the path, her arms outstretched. The king was close behind, and they lifted the baby from the cradle and smiled and hugged her and loved her.

"Our very own baby!" whispered the queen.

"Our own princess!" whispered the king.

"There!" said the willow to the roses and the lilies and the poppies and the daisies. "See how happy they are?" And he rustled his leaves proudly. The roses and lilies and poppies bowed graciously to each other and to the willow. Only the daisies wondered what had become of the thistle.

The king and the queen carried the baby tenderly into the palace.

"Now that we have our heart's desire," said the queen, "we must keep her safe from all harm."

"Indeed we must!" said the king, and he gave orders that a fence should be built all around the royal garden to keep the baby princess safe. The baby waved her little arms and cried, but the king and the queen took no notice.

Outside the fence the people of the kingdom began to murmur.

"Why does the king build such a fence? We would never harm our little princess. We wish to love her too, and to walk in the garden as we have always walked."

The children took no notice of the fence. The gardener's little boy wriggled in between the slats and the other children climbed over. They danced and sang to the baby princess, and she clapped her hands and laughed.

Summers and winters came and went, and the baby grew into a little girl. The king and the queen loved her so dearly that they spent every second of every minute of every hour watching over her.

"She is so beautiful!" smiled the queen. "She has skin as soft as rose petals!"

"She sings like the evening thrush!" laughed the king.

"She smells as sweet as the golden lilies!"

"Her eyes are as lovely as the darkness in the hearts of poppies, and as bright as the eyes of daisies!"

"She is our heart's delight," said the queen, "and nothing and nobody must ever hurt her." And she and the king gave orders that the fence should be taken down and replaced by a high wall with an iron gate.

The princess ran to the gate and pulled at it. "No!" she called. "No!" But the king ordered that it should stay.

The people beyond the wall muttered to each other. "The king and queen don't care for us any more. We used to walk among the flowers in the cool of the evening, but now they keep us out. Why should they build such a high strong wall? We love the princess too. Why should any of us hurt her?"

The children waved to the princess through the gate. Then the gardener's boy showed them how to climb on each other's backs all the way up to the top of the wall, and they hopped down into the garden.

The princess ran to the gate and pulled at it. "No!"
she called.

They played hide-and-seek and catch-as-catch-can with the princess, and she skipped and jumped and ran with them all day and every day.

Springs and autumns came and went. The princess went on growing, and the garden grew too. More and more flowers sprang up and flourished, and the royal garden became the wonder of the land. Beyond the high walls the people of the kingdom grew poorer and hungrier, but inside there were lush green tangles of scarlet-flowered creepers, and heavy hanging loops of thickly clustering orchids that smelt of cream and vanilla. The princess and the gardener's boy walked hand in hand under the arches of pink and white and deep crimson roses, and they whispered with the other children among the golden lilies. The daisies watched and nodded with their bright eyes, and the poppies dropped their silken scarlet petals on the path.

The king and the queen watched the princess and the children playing together and they shook their heads.

"Our daughter is so beautiful, so lovely. Supposing that she caught a cold, a mump or a measle from the outside children? We must love and protect her from all danger." And orders were given to build another, higher wall. Iron spikes were placed on the top, and the gates were protected with the strongest steel bars.

"Please let my friends come in," begged the princess. "Please let them come and play! Please!" But the queen and the king only patted her and smiled fondly at her.

"Come and sit under the willow," said the queen, "and I will sing to you."

"Come and walk with me in the garden," invited the king, "and I will tell you stories of long ago."

The princess looked at them. "No," she said, "no." And she went to sit curled up in the branches of the willow, and slow silver tears ran down her cheeks.

The king and the queen sighed, but they told each other it was all for the best.

"Could we ever forgive ourselves if she came to any harm?" asked the king.

"She is our everything," said the queen.

Outside the wall the people of the kingdom grew angry.

"Why do they shut out our children?" they demanded. "How can the princess be in danger from her friends? Our king and queen have always ruled us wisely and well. Have they truly forgotten us?"

The children gathered around the gates, but tall guards ordered them to go home. The gardener's youngest son struggled to climb the wall, but it was too high.

Suns and moons rose and set, and the princess grew tall and thin. She was pale now, and spent most of her days sitting beneath the willow tree, listening to the murmuring of the leaves.

"How right we were to keep those noisy children out of our garden," said the queen.

"Indeed," said the king. "They were far too rough. See how delicate and tender our princess is. She is safe here in our beautiful garden. We must make it as lovely as we can to give her pleasure. We will build fountains and waterfalls, and fill it with rare birds that sing as sweetly as the angels in heaven." And the orders were given.

Orchards were planted, full of sweet russet apples and velvet-skinned peaches and dusky plums. Sparkling fountains and tumbling waterfalls sang their rushing songs, and in the branches of all the trees gold and silver birds fluttered shining wings.

The princess grew still more pale and sad. Sometimes she walked among the roses and lilies and poppies and daisies and sighed, and sometimes she sat under the willow tree and cried until the ground was wet with her tears.

Outside the walls the children lived their lives, but they seldom laughed or danced or sang. The gardener's boy often sat outside the gates, and one or other of the children would come and sit with him. They would speak quietly of the time long ago when they had played in the garden.

\* \* \*

The king and the queen walked under the trees with the princess.

"Look at the wonderful fountains!" the queen told her.

"My friends would love to splash in the sparkling water," said the princess.

"No, no!" said the king. "Listen to the birds!"

"My friends would love to see them fly with their gold and silver wings," said the princess.

"No, no!" said the queen. "Smell the sweetness of the water lilies!"

The princess sighed and was silent.

The king suddenly stopped. *"Look!"* he said, and he pointed an angry finger. "Look! In our beautiful garden! A weed!"

The queen hurried to see. "What is it?" she asked. "Is it harmful? Will it hurt our darling? Is it dangerous?"

"It's a thistle," said the king. "Call for the gardeners! At once!"

The gardeners were called for. The thistle was taken away, but soon there was another, and then another. Professors and experts came from many distant countries to give their opinion, but whatever they did it seemed that there were always more thistles. Thistles grew among the roses and the lilies; they grew among the poppies and the daisies, and every day there were more and more and more.

"Whatever shall we do?" asked the king. "Our beautiful garden will soon be filled with thistles!"

At the steel-barred gate the gardener's boy was pleading with the guards.

"Let us in!" he begged. "Let us in, and we will pick all the thistles. We ask no reward, no payment. Only let us into the garden and all the thistles will be gone!"

The king and the queen looked up at each other.

"Did you hear?" asked the king.

The queen nodded. "Everything else in the world has been tried..."

"Children have bright eyes," said the king. "They will spy out even the smallest thistles. They can see things we cannot."

"That is true," said the queen, and she looked towards the willow tree. The princess was curled up in the branches, fast asleep. The queen sighed. "Our darling is so pale and sad. Maybe if the children pick all the thistles she will smile again."

The king stood up: "OPEN THE GATES!"

As the gates opened the children came dancing in. They skipped and hopped and ran all over the garden, picking every thistle they found. They skipped among the roses and the lilies and the poppies and the daisies, and they picked big thistles and little thistles. They hopped among the apples trees, and they picked tall thistles and small thistles. They laughed as they ran in and out and round about the royal garden, and the king and queen smiled as they watched them.

"They look so happy," said the queen. "And look, the thistles are almost gone! And no more are growing!"

The king stroked his beard. "Perhaps," he said slowly, "perhaps we were wrong to build the wall. How long is it since we heard laughter in the garden?"

The queen didn't answer. She had run to help a very small boy who had fallen among the poppies. As she picked him up he turned to her. "Pretty," he said, and as he staggered away down the path he blew the queen a kiss.

"Oh," said the queen, and her eyes were full of tears. "Oh … and we had shut them out."

The king shook his head. "We were wrong. Our princess will always be our heart's delight, but these are our children too. The children of our kingdom."

The queen put her hand on the king's shoulder. "How wise," she said. "We must order the wall to be pulled down!"

The gardener's youngest son came walking towards the king and the queen, and bowed.

"If you please," he said, "there are no more thistles. Do you wish us to leave now?"

The queen curtsied. "No," she said, "we would be honoured if you would stay."

"For ever and ever," said the king, and he turned to the guards. "As soon as you can," he ordered, "pull down the wall!"

The children cheered and laughed and threw their hats in the air, and danced hand in hand round and round the king and the queen.

"Hurrah!" they shouted. "Hurrah!"

The gardener's son bowed once more. "Thank you," he said. "And now, may we play with the princess?"

"Run and tell her that you may," said the queen, and all the children laughed again and ran to the willow tree with outstretched arms.

Up in the willow's branches the princess was still asleep.

*She's as light as down,* the old willow thought to himself, *as light as thistledown.*

And his long fingers stirred in the evening breeze.

"Princess! Princess!" The children called up from under the tree.

The princess stirred and smiled among the branches.

"Come and play! Come and play! We can play in the garden for ever and ever!"

"At last," whispered the princess. Slowly she floated upwards, up and up through the whispering leaves.

"Princess!" The children called again. "Where are you? Where are you?"

The king and the queen ran to the tree and stared and stared up into the branches. There was nothing to be seen and nothing to be heard except for the soft whispering and rustling of the leaves. The king and the queen slowly turned and moved away, and the waiting children looked at them expectantly.

"Is she still asleep?"

"Is she playing hide-and-seek?"

"Is she hiding in the garden?"

The queen shook her head. "We found her under the willow when she was a baby," she said sadly, "and now she has gone."

The king put out his hand to soothe a crying child. "You are our children now," he said. "We will comfort each other."

"And may we still play among the roses and the lilies and the daisies and the poppies?" asked a little boy.

"Of course, my darling," said the queen, and she smiled through her tears.

"For ever and ever," said the king.

The gardener's youngest son rubbed his eyes. Had he truly seen the princess drifting away through the shadows and over the garden wall? He rubbed his eyes again and said nothing, but the old willow sighed heavily.

"Willows weave beautiful cradles ... but I never will weave again."

A very small thistle growing under the willow's roots sniffed loudly. "Poof!" she said.

*She sat and stitched and sewed in a corner of the*
*kitchen and said almost nothing at all.*

# LITTLE BEEKEEPER

Once in the time of wizards there was a wizard who had three sons and one daughter. The daughter was the youngest, and no one thought very much about her. All day long she washed the clothes and cooked the meals and cleaned the house, and every evening she ran up to the apple orchard to talk to the bees in their hives. When she came back to the house she sat and stitched and sewed in a corner of the kitchen and said almost nothing at all. Her brothers called her Little Beekeeper, and the wizard fell into the habit of doing the same.

The wizard's sons were fine and strong

and handsome, but they hadn't an ounce of wizardry among them. They could cut down a tree with one swing of an axe, but they couldn't send thunderbolts hurling across the sky. They could carry enough logs on one shoulder to keep a grandmother warm all winter, but they couldn't turn the smallest prince into a toad or a toad into a prince. They could split branches into matchsticks with one hand tied behind their back, but they couldn't see faraway places in a bowl of magic water – all they could see was their own reflections, and very good-looking they thought themselves.

"Oh, dearie, dearie me!" said the wizard, and he looked at his three fine sons in despair. "Whatever will you do in life? I'm a wizard, and my father was a wizard … and I don't know anything about anything else!" And he went up into his tall tower room to think. Little Beekeeper ran up to the apple orchard where the beehives were, and whispered and whispered at the door of each hive.

*"My brothers are so strong and tall,*
*My father can't see me at all.*
*Bees, dear bees, I beg of you,*
*Tell me now what I must do!"*

*"Zzzzz! Zzzzz! Zzzzz!"* buzzed the bees, and Little Beekeeper nodded and ran back home. She picked up her broom and began sweeping the hallway.

The wizard sat in his tower room with his head in his hands. He had made enchantments and experiments and magic of every kind; he was worn out by mixing and stirring and drawing secret signs at midnight in the sand of the forest floor.

Nothing had worked; his three sons remained fine and strong and handsome, but nothing more.

The wizard sighed. "I'm growing old, and my magic is fading away. There's nothing more that I can do. They must go out into the world and seek their fortunes."

*Bang! Bang! Bang!* There was a loud knocking.

The wizard jumped up and hurried down the stairs. He pushed past Little Beekeeper and opened the door. Outside was a messenger dressed all in black, and when he saw the wizard he bowed low and handed him a letter.

"From the palace," he said, "to every household in the land."

Little Beekeeper stopped sweeping and listened.

The wizard took the letter eagerly, pulled

his spectacles from his pocket and began to read.

"Dearie, dearie me," he said to himself as he read. "The queen growing old and feeble? Dear, dear. And no prince or princess to rule the kingdom afterwards! Goodness gracious. And a competition – a competition to find a new king or queen from among the people... Well, well, *well*! Now, let me see..."

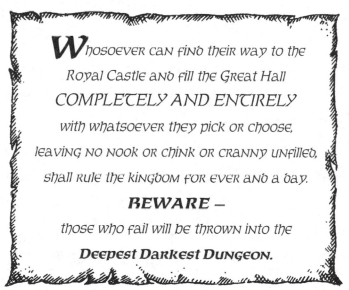

**W**hosoever can find their way to the Royal Castle and fill the Great Hall *COMPLETELY AND ENTIRELY* with whatsoever they pick or choose, leaving no nook or chink or cranny unfilled, shall rule the kingdom for ever and a day.

**BEWARE –**

those who fail will be thrown into the

**Deepest Darkest Dungeon.**

The wizard rubbed his hands together. "My boys are fine and strong and handsome. They could never fail." He folded up the letter and put it in his pocket as he went back up the stairs. Little Beekeeper went on sweeping the hallway, and she sang as she swept.

"Silence!" shouted the wizard from his tower room. Little Beekeeper stopped singing, but she smiled as she began to dust and polish.

When the three sons came rolling back from their game of skittles, the wizard told them about the competition.

"You are all strong and can work hard," he said. "Surely one of you could fill the queen's hall and become king of all the land? And then your brothers would be princes, and you would all live happily ever after."

Little Beekeeper listened as she stitched away at a pile of holey socks but she said nothing. Her three brothers laughed and joked and banged each other on the back.

"No one is as strong as us!" they boasted. "One of us will become king before the week is out!" Then they began to argue about which of them should go first, and what they would do as soon as they were made king. They argued so loudly and for so long that at last the wizard called up all his strength and sent a thunderbolt to silence them.

"I know!" shouted the youngest son as he picked himself up from the floor. "We'll ask Little Beekeeper who should go first!" And he pointed to his sister, sitting and sewing in her corner.

"She knows nothing about anything!" said the middle son. "Why, she's good for nothing but looking after the bees!"

"Then let her ask the bees which of us should go first!" said the oldest son, and he pulled Little Beekeeper out of her corner and pushed her out of the door. Up to the apple orchard she ran, and whispered and whispered at the door of each hive.

*"Bees, dear bees, I beg of you,*
*Tell me now what I should do!"*

*"Zzzzz! Zzzzz! Zzzzz!"* buzzed the bees, and Little Beekeeper pointed. Then she hurried back to the kitchen.

*"Well?"* shouted her brothers. Little Beekeeper nodded at the oldest.

"I said she was good for nothing," grumbled the middle brother.

"She's good for nothing at all," complained the youngest, but the oldest was already pulling on his coat.

\* \* \*

*She whispered at the door of each hive.*

The wizard's oldest son marched along the road to the queen's castle. As he went he swung his axe round and round his head and thought about how he would soon be king.

"I shall play skittles every day," he said to himself, "and my skittles will be made of silver." And he laughed as he strode up the steps to the castle door and banged on the knocker as loudly as he could.

The door was opened by a little old woman dressed all in black.

The oldest son looked her up and down. "When I live here," he announced, "I shall have soldiers dressed in red and purple to answer the door." And he pushed past the old woman and stared rudely about him.

"I've come to be king, old leatherface," he said. "Show me the hall, and I'll fill it!"

The old woman smiled, and her little black eyes glittered and shone.

"Come this way, my young and foolish boy," she said, and she led the oldest son along a dark and winding corridor. At the end she threw open a heavy door studded with iron nails. The oldest son strode through, and then stopped. He was standing in the most enormous hall he had ever seen. It was truly vast. The soaring arched roof rose up and up and up above the dirty and flaking walls, and the blackened floor stretched away and away in front of him. The tall windows were coated with dust and laced with spiders' webs, and the light that came in was dim and grey.

"Oh," said the oldest son, looking all about him. "Ah."

"You have three days and three nights," said the old woman. "You may come and you may go for those three days and nights, but if at the end the great hall is not filled completely and entirely, every nook and chink and cranny, then you will be thrown into the deepest dungeon for ever and ever and ever." And she turned round and shuffled away.

The oldest son shook himself. "Well," he said, "I'd be better beginning than standing here and staring. After all, I can cut down a tree with one swing of my axe. I'll soon have this hall filled completely and entirely." He rushed out of the hall and back the way he had come. He burst out of the castle door, and as he hurried into the forest he was already swinging his axe above his head. He chose the tallest tree and felled it with one blow.

"H'mph," he said to himself as he hauled and heaved the tree trunk round the corners of the corridor. "When I am king I'll have this castle pulled right down and build myself a marvellous and magnificent palace." And he pulled the tree into the hall and went back for another, and another, and another.

At the end of the three days and nights the oldest son had filled the great hall. Tree trunks were heaped high and branches and twigs piled above them, up to the arches of the roof. Leaves littered the floor. The oldest son lay, puffing and panting, in the doorway.

The old woman came shuffling up.

"Well, well, well," she said. "So you think you have filled the hall completely and entirely?"

"That I have, old bag and baggage," said the oldest son. "Now, give me my crown!"

"Not so fast," said the old woman, and she clapped her hands. A flock of white pigeons came fluttering all around her, cooing and clucking and murmuring.

"Fly, my little dears!" the old woman told them. "Fly! Find me any nooks and chinks and crannies!"

The pigeons flapped their wings and rose up into the air like a scattering of white petals. They flew in and out of the tree trunks, they perched among the branches, they paddled up and down among the leaves.

"Ho, ho, ho!" The old woman cackled delightedly. "No crown for you, my fine and foolish fellow!" And she clapped her hands a second time. The pigeons swooped down and touched her cheek with their soft wings, and then fluttered away. As they left the hall there was the crunch of marching feet. Six silver soldiers came wheeling round from the corridor. They seized the oldest son as if he weighed less than a feather, and although he struggled and shouted they carried him off and away down to the deepest dungeon in the castle.

As the heavy wooden door swung shut there was a flash and a bang. A wisp of purple smoke floated up. The oldest son felt himself shrinking and shrinking, and his skin wrinkled and turned greenish yellowish brown. He tried to shout for help.

"Croak! Croak! Croak!" was all he could say. "Croak! Croak! Croak!"

No one answered, and he was left with a heap of wet hay to sleep under and a crust of bread to eat.

The old wizard, the two remaining brothers and Little Beekeeper waited and waited for the oldest son to come marching home in triumph. At last the wizard shook his head and went to try his spells over a bowl of magic water. *Abracadabra!* There was the deepest darkest dungeon of the castle, and there was the oldest son's coat hanging on a rusty nail. *Fsss-sss-ss!* The picture clouded over.

"Oh, dearie," said the wizard. "My poor, poor boy! Will we ever see him again?"

The second brother snorted. "Serves him right. Now it's *my* turn to go. I'll be crowned king before the end of the week!" He pulled on his hat, snatched up his axe and set out along the road, whistling and singing as he went.

"When I am king," he said to himself, "I shall play skittles every day, and my skittles will be made of solid gold."

The second son knocked on the castle door, and the old woman dressed all in black opened it.

*"Well!"* said the second son, staring at her. "When I am king the door will be opened by a string of servants, all dressed in scarlet silks and satins. Show me the great hall, old raggle taggle. I have come to be made king!"

The old woman smiled, and her little black eyes glittered and shone.

"Come with me," she said, "my young and foolish boy," and she led him along the winding passage to the great hall.

The hall was empty and echoing. The second son looked all around him, his eyes popping wide with amazement.

"You have three days and three nights," said the old woman. "You may come and you may go for those three days and nights, but if at the end the great hall is not filled completely and entirely, every nook and chink and cranny, then you will be thrown into the deepest dungeon for ever and ever

51

*"Show me the great hall, old raggle taggle. I have come to be made king!"*

and ever." And she turned round and shuffled away.

The second son rubbed his head. "I'd best get busy," he said to himself, and he shouldered his axe and hurried outside. At the edge of the forest he stopped. In front of him was a mighty heap of tree trunks and branches and twigs and leaves, piled high and seeming to reach almost to the sky.

"This looks like my brother's work," said the second son, "and very handy it will be!" And he began to chop the tree trunks and branches into logs. When he had built a stack he swung them onto his shoulder and carried them into the great hall. In two days and nights he had used up all the wood his brother had cut, and he hastily cut more and more and more from the forest trees. At the end of three days and nights the great hall was filled to the very rafters, and the second brother lay puffing and panting in the doorway.

The old woman came shuffling up.

"Well, well, well," she said. "So you think you have filled the hall completely and entirely?"

"Can't you see that I have, old tortoise?" said the second son. "Bring me my crown!"

"Not so fast," said the old woman, and she clapped her hands. A drift of butterflies came floating down around her, their wings shining in the dim and dusty air.

"Go, my pretties!" The old woman waved them towards the logs. "See if you can find me any nooks and chinks and crannies!"

The butterflies flew up and up and up. They flittered in and out between the logs, and they settled and opened and closed their bright wings in every space.

"Ho, ho, ho!" The old woman shook with

laughter. "No crown for you, my fine and foolish fellow!" And again she clapped her hands. The butterflies drifted away, brushing her cheeks with their painted wings as they went. The six silver soldiers came marching down the corridor. The second son found himself picked up as if he weighed nothing at all. In no time he was bundled into the deepest darkest dungeon.

As the heavy wooden door swung shut there was a flash and a bang. A wisp of orange smoke floated up. The second son felt himself shrinking and shrinking, and his skin wrinkled and turned greenish yellowish brown.

"Croak! Croak!" said a large fat toad in the corner.

The second son looked up. "Croak," he said, and he hopped across to steal the crust of bread.

* * *

The old wizard, the third son and Little Beekeeper waited and waited for the second son to come marching home in triumph. At last the wizard sighed and went to look in his bowl of magic water. The water was misty and cloudy, and the wizard groaned.

"My magic is all used up!" he said, but as he muttered spell after spell the water slowly cleared. *Abracadabra!* There was the oldest son's coat still hanging on the dungeon wall, and there beside it was the second son's hat.

"Poor, poor boys!" said the wizard sadly.

"My turn now!" said the youngest son. "I'm *sure* to be made king! I'm the finest, the strongest, the handsomest of us all!" And he tucked his axe into his belt and set off along the road, humming cheerfully.

"When I'm king," he said to himself, "I shall play skittles all day with a ball made of diamonds and rubies!"

The youngest son knocked so hard on the castle door that sparks flew in the air.

"You'll have to be off, old brittlebones," he told the old woman in black. "I'm to be king here, and I'll have knights in golden armour to open the door for me. Now, take me to the hall!"

The old woman led the youngest son down the long winding corridor. She smiled as she walked in front of him, and her little black eyes glittered and shone.

"You have three days and three nights," she told him. "You may come and you may go for those three days and nights, but if at the end the great hall is not filled completely and entirely, every nook and chink and cranny, then you will be thrown into the deepest dungeon for ever and ever and ever." And she turned round and shuffled away.

The youngest son hardly listened. He was pacing out the length and the width of the floor, and squinting up into the dusty arched roof.

"H'mph!" he said. "It'll be hard work, but it can be done!" And when he found the enormous heap of logs at the edge of the forest he nodded. "Just what I need!" he said, and set to work splitting them into the finest of matchsticks.

As the three days and nights went by, the youngest son worked faster and faster. He ran to and fro filling the hall with armfuls of matchsticks. At the last minute he pushed the final sliver of wood into place.

"Not a chink or a nook or a cranny that isn't filled!" he gasped, and fell down in the doorway puffing and panting.

"We'll see about that," said the old woman as she shuffled up beside him. "We'll see!"

and she clapped her hands.

A black wave of tiny ants came flooding down the corridor. The old woman nodded to them.

"My tiny ones, creep and climb and crawl! Find all the chinks and nooks and crannies!"

The ants scattered in among the matchstick slivers of wood. They crept and they climbed and they crawled in among the chinks and the nooks and the crannies, and the old woman rocked with laughter.

"Ho, ho, ho! No crown for you, my fine and foolish fellow!" And she clapped her hands together until all the ants had crawled back through the wooden matchsticks and were gathered at her feet. They swirled around her, and then scurried away as the six silver soldiers came marching up the corridor.

* * *

As the heavy wooden door swung shut on the youngest son there was the brightest flash of all. A cloud of green smoke floated up, and the youngest son coughed as he felt himself shrinking and shrinking.

"Croak! Croak! Croak!" said the two fat toads in the corner, and they watched as the youngest son's skin wrinkled and turned greenish yellowish brown. The youngest son tried to cough again, but he could only croak. He sat and glared angrily at the two fat toads, and they glared back. On the dungeon wall the youngest son's belt hung beside the coat and the hat.

The old wizard and Little Beekeeper waited and waited for the youngest son to come marching home in triumph. The wizard creaked his way up to his room and peered

*The wizard ... peered into his bowl of magic water, but it was green and weedy and he could see nothing at all.*

into his bowl of magic water, but it was green and weedy and he could see nothing at all.

"My poor, poor boys," he said, and he sighed heavily. "Will I ever see them again?"

Little Beekeeper stood up. "Now, Father," she said, "it is my turn to go to the castle."

"*You?*" said the wizard. "What can *you* do?" And he went up into his tall tower room to stare sadly out over the forest.

Little Beekeeper smiled, but she said nothing. She picked up a plate, a spoon and a basket and went out to the apple orchard. When she came back the plate was heaped with honeycomb, and the basket was full of beeswax. She covered the honey with a cloth, and for the rest of the day she cleaned and softened and smoothed the wax. When the evening star began to climb the pale silver sky she pulled three long hairs from her head, and twisted and plaited them together. As the moon followed the star up and up into the velvet night Little Beekeeper spun the soft yellow wax round and round and round the twist of hair, until by the time the moon sank down once more at the other end of night she had made a tall and golden candle.

As the sun rose Little Beekeeper knocked on her father's door.

"Father," she said, "I've come to say goodbye."

The wizard stroked his beard. "Don't go, Little Beekeeper," he said. "Who will wash the clothes and cook the meals and clean the house? Don't go."

Little Beekeeper shook her head. "The bees are waiting to show me the way." She ran down the stairs and into the kitchen. She picked up the plate of honeycomb and carefully wrapped the tall golden candle in her shawl. Outside the door the bees were buzzing and humming in a quivering cloud, and as Little Beekeeper stepped out they flew up into the air and led her away down the path through the forest.

When Little Beekeeper reached the castle she climbed slowly up the steps and knocked gently at the door. The bees flew high in the air as the old woman dressed all in black came out. Little Beekeeper curtsied down to the ground, and held out the plate of honey.

"Madam," she said, "I bring you a present."

The old woman smiled, and her eyes were bright and shining.

"Thank you, my child," she said. "Will you rest a little after your journey?"

Little Beekeeper curtsied again. "If you

please, I should like to see the great hall."

The old woman took Little Beekeeper by the hand and led her down the long winding corridor into the vast and empty cavern of the hall.

"You have three days and three nights, my dear. You may come and you may go for those three days and nights, but if at the end the great hall is not filled completely and entirely, every nook and chink and cranny, then you will be thrown into the deepest dungeon for ever and ever and ever. But, dear child – why don't you run away home and be safe for ever and a day?"

Little Beekeeper touched her arm gently. "Thank you," she said, "but I must stay."

The old woman nodded, and shuffled away.

As soon as the old woman had gone Little Beekeeper looked all around her. She saw the cobwebs and the flaking walls and the dim grey light. Then she sat down on the blackened and dirty floor in the very centre of the hall, her shawl in her lap. There she sat, for three days and three nights. Every night at midnight the old woman came and asked if there was anything she wished for, but Little Beekeeper only smiled and shook her head.

At midnight on the third night the castle bell tolled twelve long strokes. There was no glimmer of light coming through the tall dusty windows, and the great hall was as black as night's own shadow. Little Beekeeper stirred, and stood up. She unwrapped the tall golden candle and placed it on the floor. She took a tinderbox from her pocket, struck a spark and lit the candle. The flame flickered for a moment, and then burnt straight and tall and golden.

Light welled up, and the darkness fled away. The whole of the great hall glowed warm and yellow molten gold.

Little Beekeeper walked slowly to the iron studded door and opened it. The old woman was standing on the other side. As she saw the great hall filled with light, she cried out and clapped her hands.

At once a swarm of bees came buzzing and humming and bumbling all about her.

"Fly, fly, my precious ones," said the old woman. "Fly and search the great hall. See if it is filled completely and entirely."

The bees flew up and around the hall. They flew this way and that, they flew high and they flew low, but wherever they flew the golden light of Little Beekeeper's candle shone.

"*Zzzz! Zzzz! Zzzz!*" buzzed the bees, and they circled round Little Beekeeper's head.

"Every nook and chink and cranny is full of light," said the old woman. "At last the great hall is filled, completely and entirely." And she clapped her hands one last time.

Six silver soldiers came marching, marching down the long winding corridor. They were carrying cloaks of silk and satin and velvet, and a crown of silver and gold glittering with diamonds and rubies. The old woman swung one cloak round her own shoulders, and the other she wrapped around Little Beekeeper. She took the crown, and placed it on Little Beekeeper's head.

"Be queen, my dear," she said, "and be happy."

There was a roaring of trumpets and a crashing of drums. Suddenly the great hall was filled with people, all cheering for their new queen. The floor was polished silver, and the walls were shining gold, and diamonds twinkled in the glittering arches of the roof. At the end of the hall was a golden throne studded with rubies, and the old queen took Little Beekeeper by the hand and led her to her rightful place.

And what happened then? What of the wizard and the three brothers?

The feasting and rejoicing went on for days and days and days, but the brothers and the wizard knew nothing about it. At last a messenger arrived at the wizard's house, carefully carrying a bowl of water.

"A gift from the queen, sire," he said.

The wizard took the bowl and peered into it. He saw a picture in its clear depths, a picture of Little Beekeeper dressed in royal robes and wearing a gold and silver crown. He saw her raise her hand and send a thunderbolt flashing up and up into the roof of the great hall. It exploded with a crash, and purple and orange and green stars scattered and flew in every direction.

The wizard jumped up in amazement, and upset the bowl of magic water.

In the deep dark dungeon the three toads leapt into the air with a yell. Stars lit up the darkness and the door to the dungeon swung wide open. Croaking loudly, the three fat toads hopped out and off and away down the forest path.

One autumn day the six silver soldiers brought the wizard a thousand sacks of matchsticks. He never knew who sent them, but he burnt them on his fire and they kept him warm all the winter. He often sat staring into the flames, wondering what had become of his three fine sons. Sometimes he sat there all night long while the matchsticks crackled and burned and glowed. It was difficult for him to sleep. Every night it was the same – three loud toads croaking and croaking and croaking all night long outside his window…

*He had nothing that belonged to him ... but he sang
and he whistled as he worked.*

# TOMKIN AND THE
# THREE LEGGED STOOL

There was once a little tailor called Tomkin. He had no mother, no father, no brothers and no sisters. He had nothing that belonged to him except for his needles, his reels of cotton, his scissors, and a three legged stool, but he sang and he whistled as he worked.

One night Tomkin had a dream. He dreamed that instead of eating hard bread and water for his supper he had hot cabbage soup with soft white rolls. He dreamed that instead of sleeping on a cold and draughty bench he had a warm and cosy bed with thick red blankets. He dreamed that instead of sitting all day on a little wooden stool with three legs he sat on a golden throne...

Tomkin sat up on his bench and rubbed his eyes.

"Well!" he said. "That was a good dream – the best I've ever had. Hot cabbage soup! Thick red blankets! And me a king – whatever can it mean?" He scratched his head, and looked at his three legged stool.

"What do you think?" he asked.

The three legged stool turned around twice and bowed.

"I think Your Majesty should go out and find your kingdom," it said.

"You're quite right," said Tomkin. "All I do here is mend shirts and stockings and sew on the mayor's buttons twice a week. I'll be off right away." He hopped off the bench and packed a bag with all his needles, three reels of cotton and a pair of sharp scissors.

"Now I'm ready," he said, but he didn't go out through the door.

"What are you waiting for?" asked the three legged stool.

"I was wondering if I'd be lonely, travelling all the way to my kingdom on my own," said Tomkin.

"It might be near, or it might be far," said the three legged stool. "Shall I come with you?"

"Yes, please," said Tomkin, "and when I'm king I promise I'll make you prime minister."

The stool spun round on one leg and sang:

*"Promises, promises, one, two, three,*
*A king will never remember me."*

"Oh, yes, I will," said Tomkin, and they went through the door together.

* * *

Tomkin walked along the road with a hop, a skip and a jump, and the three legged stool trundled along beside him. They walked through a forest and over a hill and down into the valley on the other side. Sometimes they talked, and sometimes they were silent, and sometimes Tomkin whistled a tune and the stool danced on its three wooden legs.

Down in the valley was a wide river and Tomkin and the three legged stool came to a stop.

"Oh, dear," said Tomkin, "I can't swim! Do you think my kingdom is on this side or the other side of the river?"

"It might be far, or it might be near," said the stool. "But as to swimming – just throw me in and hold on tightly!"

Tomkin waded into the rushing water, holding on to the stool. The current caught him and swirled him off his feet, but the wooden stool bobbed and floated on top of the water.

"*Oof!*" spluttered Tomkin, and he kicked and splashed until he and the stool were on the far side of the river. They staggered up the bank, and sat down to rest.

"You're a very good swimmer," Tomkin said to the three legged stool. "And when I'm king I promise I'll make you prime minister."

The stool spun round on two legs and sang:

*"Promises, promises, one, two, three,*
*A king will never remember me."*

"Yes, I will," said Tomkin indignantly.

Tomkin and the stool walked on and on, and as they walked they noticed that the grass and bushes on either side of the path were dusty brown. The trees had no leaves and the earth was hard and cracked.

"It looks as if it hasn't rained here for ages and ages," said Tomkin. "But it must be going to rain soon – look at the sky!"

The sky was leaden grey, and a huge black cloud was swirling round the top of the hill ahead of them. They could see a village halfway up the hill, and beyond the village was a castle.

"Maybe that's my kingdom," Tomkin said.

"Maybe it is," said the stool. "It certainly looks as if all the people have come out to meet us."

Tomkin stopped and stared. The three legged stool was quite right – many men and women and children were hurrying down the hill towards them.

Tomkin shook his head. "I don't think I

want to be king here," he said. "All these people look as sad as sad can be."

A bony little girl reached Tomkin and the three legged stool first.

"Oh, please!" she gasped, clutching at Tomkin's arm. "Please – have you come to make it rain?"

"What?" Tomkin said. "What do you mean? There's the biggest blackest cloud I ever saw over there – it must be about to rain puddles and ponds and lakes and seas any moment now."

The little girl began to sob and to cry, although not one tear came out of her eyes.

"But that's just it!" she wailed. "The cloud is always there – but it never, ever rains! All our rivers have dried up, and we've had no water now for days and weeks and months. Our cows and sheep have run away, and we have nothing left to eat but one cupful of flour. All our fields are dry and bare except for one small cabbage. And if it doesn't rain soon, we will all dry up into dust and blow away in the wind."

Tomkin looked around him at all the people. They were gazing at him, their eyes huge and hopeful in their thin pinched faces. He looked up at the black cloud, and he shifted his bag on his back and rubbed his nose.

"Well…" he said.

"Ahem," said the three legged stool in a small voice beside him. "Doesn't that cloud look full of rain? As full of rain as a bag might be full of needles and reels of cotton … but one snip from your scissors and they'd all fall out!"

"*Oh!*" said Tomkin. "Oh, yes! How clever you are – when I'm king I'm certainly going

*"If it doesn't rain soon, we will all dry up into dust and blow away in the wind."*

to make you prime minister!"

The stool spun round on three legs and sang:

*"Promises, promises, one, two, three,*
*A king will never remember me!"*

"Just you wait and see!" said Tomkin, and he marched on along the path and up the hill.

"Be careful!" the stool called after him. "A little can go a very long way!"

"I know what I'm doing," said Tomkin.

Up and up he went; past the village and past the castle until he was at the top of the hill and the huge black cloud was billowing just above his head. Tomkin swung the bag off his back and pulled out his scissors.

"Look at me!" he shouted.

*Snip! Snap! Rip!* Tomkin cut three long slashes right across the cloud. WHOOSH! the rush of rain washed him off his feet and sent him gasping and tumbling all the way back down to the bottom of the hill.

"HURRAH! HURRAH! HURRAH!" shouted the men and the women and the children, and they danced round and round in the silver sheets of pouring rain. They laughed and they sang and they cried and they cheered, and they picked up Tomkin and carried him back up the hill to the castle.

"You must be our king!" they said, and they sat him on a golden throne and put a golden crown on his head. They fetched him hot cabbage soup and soft white rolls, and they showed him his bed heaped with thick red blankets.

At the bottom of the hill the three legged stool stood and waited for Tomkin. It stood there with the rain beating down on it, and a cold wind blowing about it. In a small, sad voice it sang:

*"Promises, promises, one, two, three,*
*When will the king remember me?"*

It went on raining. It rained without stopping, day and night, night and day. The trees and the fields grew green, and then became dark and heavy with the never-ending rain. Up in the castle Tomkin laughed and danced and sang, but as the rains went on he watched the rivers begin to flow again, and then fill and fill until they flooded their banks and rushed and gushed all over the countryside. The men and the women and the children stopped being happy and began to complain.

"What's the use of rain if it never stops?" they asked each other. "We were unhappy before, but if the floods wash our village away we'll be even worse off." And they walked up the path to the castle and demanded to see King Tomkin.

"You must stop the rain and bring back the sun," they said. "If you can't, we'll take away your crown and send you off on your travels again."

"Oh, dear," said Tomkin. "Well – maybe I could sew the holes together."

He put his bag on his back and walked out of the castle and up to the top of the hill with the villagers following behind him. The black cloud was still in the sky, but it had poured out so much water that it was now high up, and far beyond his reach. Tomkin rubbed his nose.

"I need a ladder," he said. "I need lots of ladders."

"Then will you make it stop raining?" asked a little boy.

Tomkin nodded. "I'll try," he said.

"Hurrah!" shouted the little boy. "King Tomkin is going to mend the cloud!"

All the men and women and children from the village went hurrying off through the rain to fetch their ladders. They fetched their tables, and they fetched their chairs, and they heaped them one on top of the other into a tower that rose higher and higher.

"It's not high enough," Tomkin said. "What else have you got?"

They brought out beds and baths and chests of drawers. They carried dressers and cupboards and baskets and buckets and boxes, and piled them up and up.

"Is there anything else?" asked Tomkin.

"Nothing," said the villagers, staring at the tottering tower and shaking their dripping heads. "There's not so much as a bead box left to bring."

"All right," said Tomkin. "Now I'll see what I can do." And he began to climb.

Up went Tomkin, pulling himself up the ladders and climbing up and over the cupboards and chairs. Soon he could see the world around him for miles and miles, and still he climbed up and up. The big black cloud grew closer and closer, and he shook the rain from his eyes and kept on climbing.

Tomkin reached the top of the tower. He stood on the highest chair and stretched upwards ... and he couldn't reach. He could see the three long splits in the cloud, but he was just too far away to touch them.

"I can't do it!" Tomkin said. "I can't reach."

The villagers began to whisper to each other and to mutter and to growl.

*Tomkin looked down. He saw the rain-soaked fields,
and the rippling floodwater creeping closer.*

"Throw down your crown, Tomkin!" they shouted. "You're no king of ours! Throw down your crown, and be on your way!"

Tomkin looked down. He saw the cold, miserable villagers, and he saw that all their tables and chairs and cupboards and beds and boxes were wet and spoiled. He saw the rain-soaked fields, and the rippling flood-water creeping closer and closer to the village. And far, far off, at the bottom of the path, he saw the three legged stool patiently waiting for him.

Tomkin took a deep breath. "I cut the cloud too deeply and I've made it rain for ever and ever," he said. "And I forgot my oldest friend. I don't deserve to be a king," and he tossed the crown to the ground. His tears dropped down and mixed with the streams of water flowing down the hill …

down to the three legged stool.

Up jumped the stool, and hurried up the hill.

"Stop!" it called. "Wait for me!" And it scurried through the groups of wailing villagers to the bottom of the tower. Tomkin was sitting at the top with his head in his hands, but when he heard the stool calling he sat up straight and wiped his eyes.

Everyone watched the stool scrambling up the tower. Up and up it went, and when it reached the top Tomkin held it steady.

"I'm so sorry I forgot you," he said. "I really, truly am."

"No time for that now," said the stool as it balanced itself on top of the very topmost chair. "Come along – climb on me."

Tomkin took his needles and thread out of his bag, and climbed on the stool. He was just high enough to reach the three long rips in the cloud and he began to sew. He sewed all day long without stopping once, and gradually the rain grew less and less, until by the evening there was only a fine mist in the air.

"A couple more stitches and I'll be done," said Tomkin.

"That's good," said the stool.

Tomkin stopped suddenly.

"Oh!" he said. "Oh, no!"

"What's the matter?" asked the stool.

"It's no good," Tomkin said, "it's no good at all. There are needle holes in the cloud at the beginning and end of every stitch. I can see thousands of water drops squeezing through them – I'll *never* be able to stop the rain."

"Nobody wants you to stop the rain for ever," said the stool. "Finish your stitching."

"But it's no good," Tomkin said. "The

whole village will be washed away, and it's all my fault." He made his last stitch and pulled it tight.

"Well done," said the stool. "Now look!"

Tomkin looked. The setting sun had come creeping out from behind the cloud and was shining through the mist. A rainbow was shimmering from one side of the hill to the other, and the puddles and ponds and lakes were shining golden mirrors of light.

"KING TOMKIN! KING TOMKIN!" called the villagers. "Come down and take up your crown!"

Tomkin shook his head, and began climbing down the tower with the three legged stool close behind him. Halfway down, a gust of wind blew a flurry of raindrops against Tomkin's face.

"Why!" he said. "The rain's like silver

needles! It must be blowing through the needle holes in the cloud – but it isn't rushing and gushing like it was before."

"That's right," said the stool. "But a little can go a very long way."

Tomkin reached the ground, picked up the crown and handed it to the oldest villager.

"I'm not fit to be a king," he said, "but if you want someone wise and clever I think you should ask the three legged stool."

The villager bowed to the stool, and the stool bowed back.

"A king," said the stool, "should always know when he's made a mistake."

"Quite so," said the oldest villager.

"And a king should be willing to work all day without stopping for the good of his people," said the stool.

"My thoughts exactly," said the oldest

villager.

"And a king should be as happy when he has nothing but a bag of needles as when he has a golden throne."

"I couldn't have put it better myself," said the oldest villager, and he picked up the golden crown and handed it back to Tomkin.

"Hurrah for King Tomkin!" shouted all the villagers.

Tomkin held up his hand and the men and the women and the children were silent.

"Thank you very much," he said, and he bowed. "But I will only be king if the three legged stool is prime minister."

"It will be my pleasure," said the three legged stool.

"Hurrah for the three legged stool! Three cheers for our prime minister! And three more cheers for our wonderful king!" and the villagers picked Tomkin up and carried him off to the castle.

The three legged stool and the oldest villager walked up the path together.

"The best king of all," said the oldest villager, "is a king who keeps his promises."

And the stool sang:

*"Promises, promises, one, two, three,*
*This is the king for you and me!"*

and he followed Tomkin into the castle with a hop, a skip and a jump.

THE

END